A NOTE TO PARENTS AND CAREGIVERS

Epilepsy can be a frightening and confusing disease, especially for children. Not only is the disease difficult to understand, but the process of visiting the neurologist and taking EEGs, MRIs, and blood tests can also be scary for young children as they first learn about their epilepsy. Taking an epilepsy medication regularly may also be an adjustment. In addition, children with epilepsy may feel isolated or afraid that they might have a seizure at any time.

As a practicing physician for thirty years and the founder of numerous health care facilities, I have learned that children have a natural curiosity and a resilience that often surprises adults. Children want and need clear explanations and straight answers to gain a sense of control over their own lives. Many parents struggle with telling their children about epilepsy. Often, parents don't know how to explain the disease simply and succinctly. Sometimes, parents and caregivers provide different explanations that can cause a young child to worry. By reading this book along with a child in a medical facility, in a school, or in the home, parents and caregivers can present a standard message about epilepsy that is both educational and reassuring.

All of us want to give children with epilepsy the knowledge, confidence, and strength they need to live happy, healthy, and normal lives. I hope that this story of superhero Katie Kate and the Worry Wombat will allow you and your child to create and maintain a positive, joyful, and open attitude about epilepsy.

—M. Maitland DeLand, M.D.

For Andrew

Published by Greenleaf Book Group Press
Austin, Texas
www.gbgpress.com

Distributed by Greenleaf Book Group LLC

For ordering information or special discounts for bulk purchases, please contact
Greenleaf Book Group LLC at PO Box 91869, Austin, TX 78709, 512.891.6100.

Design and composition by Greenleaf Book Group LLC
Cover design by Greenleaf Book Group LLC
Illustrations by Jennifer Zivoin

Publisher's Cataloging-In-Publication Data (Prepared by The Donohue Group, Inc.)

DeLand, M. Maitland.
The Great Katie Kate. Explains epilepsy / M. Maitland DeLand ; with illustrations by Jennifer Zivoin. — 1st ed.
p. : ill. ; cm.

Issued also as an ebook.
Summary: When Jimmy is diagnosed with epilepsy, the Great Katie Kate swoops
in to help alleviate his fears brought on by the Worry Wombat.
ISBN: 978-1-62634-007-7

1. Epilepsy in children--Juvenile fiction. 2. Epilepsy--Patients—Juvenile fiction. 3. Children—Preparation for medical care—Juvenile fiction. 4. Superheroes—Juvenile fiction. 5. Epilepsy—Patients—Fiction. 6. Children—Preparation for medical care—Fiction. 7. Superheroes—Fiction. I. Zivoin, Jennifer. II. Title. III. Title: Great Katie Kate explains epilepsy

PZ7.D37314 Gre 2014
[E]   2013943708

Part of the Tree Neutral® program, which offsets the number of trees consumed in the production and printing of this book by taking proactive steps, such as planting trees in direct proportion to the number of trees used: www.treeneutral.com.

Manufactured by Imago on acid-free paper
Manufactured in Singapore, August 2013
Batch No. 1

13 14 15 16 17   10 9 8 7 6 5 4 3 2 1
First Edition

THE Great Katie Kate

EXPLAINS EPILEPSY

M. Maitland DeLand, M.D.

with illustrations by Jennifer Zivoin

GREENLEAF
BOOK GROUP PRESS

One night, as Jimmy was sound asleep, his trusty dog Bjorn began barking. Bjorn was very concerned. Something was wrong.

Jimmy's mother heard Bjorn barking and ran into Jimmy's room. "What's wrong, Bjorn?" she asked. Then she saw why the dog was worried.

Jimmy was in his bed, but he was shaking and he didn't seem to hear Bjorn at all. He was covered in sweat. "Jimmy, what's happening?" his mother cried. But Jimmy didn't answer.

Jimmy's mother called for help right away. This was not the first time that she had found Jimmy shaking and unable to hear her ask if he was okay. It was time to see the doctor to find out what was wrong.

Bjorn barked again. "Don't worry," Jimmy's mother said. "I called an ambulance."

Jimmy woke up in a hospital bed in the emergency room.

"What happened to me?" Jimmy asked. "I don't remember coming here. I started to feel funny and I tried to call out to Bjorn, but I couldn't even remember his name. After that, I don't remember anything."

"You had a seizure," the doctor said in a reassuring voice. "To help us find out why, I'm going to send you to a neurologist."

A seizure? A neurologist? Jimmy began to worry.

Jimmy's mom held his hand. "I'm right here, Jimmy."

A nice nurse took Jimmy down the hall to the neurologist's office. In the waiting room, Jimmy sat down on the floor next to some other kids who were playing.

Just then, a whirling ball of energy blasted into the room. Jimmy covered his eyes.

When Jimmy opened his eyes, he saw a small redheaded girl in a cape. She had freckles across her nose and a giant, bright smile.

"Hello, Jimmy, I'm The Great Katie Kate. I'm here to help you understand what happened to you and why you're here."

"But I don't know what's happening, and I'm really worried," Jimmy told her.

"Since you had some seizures, you might have a special condition called epilepsy. I'm going to tell you all about it. See that Worry Wombat hiding over there?" Katie Kate pointed to a furry creature that was hanging out near the magazine rack.

"The Worry Wombat?" Jimmy asked.

"The Worry Wombat shows up when kids get worried. But all you have to do is ask questions and learn as much as you can about why you're in the hospital, and he'll take a hike."

Jimmy smiled. "He looks funny."

"Oh, he's a real character!" said Katie Kate. "Now let's get started learning more about epilepsy."

"The first thing to remember," Katie Kate told Jimmy, "is that lots of kids have epilepsy. As many as one in twenty-five kids have it. And there are different kinds of epilepsy and different kinds of seizures. Isn't that right, Susan?"

Susan nodded and smiled. "One morning I was combing my hair when my arms started jerking. Then they stopped. Later, when I was eating breakfast, it happened again. I got milk all over me."

"It sounds like you had myoclonic seizures, Susan," said Katie Kate.

"I was playing tag with my friends," said a boy named Michael. "I don't remember this, but they said I just stopped running and stared into space for a little while. They couldn't get me to talk or move. Then I just started playing again. The same thing happened later on when I was baking cookies with my mom. So she brought me to the neurologist."

"Michael, you probably had an absence seizure," said The Great Katie Kate.

Next, Eddie told his story. "I was sitting in class and suddenly the teacher's voice sounded funny, like she was talking under water. Later on, I started to hear a strange ringing sound, but nobody else could hear it," he said.

"Some seizures don't affect your muscles," said Katie Kate. "Eddie, you may have had a sensory seizure."

"I wasn't feeling well at school," said a girl named Cindy. "On my way to the nurse's office, I started to feel funny and my muscles got stiff. I think I fell down, but I don't really remember. My friends said that I was jerking around on the floor. I woke up in the emergency room."

"Cindy, it sounds like you had a tonic-clonic seizure," said Katie Kate. "Isn't that a funny-sounding name?"

"I see that people have different kinds of seizures," Jimmy said. "But what causes a seizure?"

"I'm glad you asked, Jimmy. Let's explore the human brain. Do you know what the brain does?" asked Katie Kate.

"Yes, the brain helps you think," Jimmy said.

"That's right. But the brain does a whole lot more than that. Some parts of your brain control your muscles. Some parts control your senses: how you see, hear, smell, taste, and feel. Other parts help you talk and remember things."

"Like how I remember my dog's name—Bjorn."

"Exactly."

"Your brain is like a huge computer, processing lots of information and sending signals to your body. So when something goes wrong in your brain, unusual signals get sent to your body.

Your muscles might get stiff or start jerking, you may forget where you are or what you're doing, or you might smell or hear strange things. You might accidentally go to the bathroom. When something like that happens, we call it a seizure. And if you have seizures, you could have epilepsy."

"But I don't want to have seizures. What if it happens at school? I'll be so embarrassed," Jimmy said, with a worried frown.

"Don't worry, Jimmy," Katie Kate said. "There are lots of people with epilepsy. And I'll tell you about all of the things you can do to help prevent seizures."

Next, The Great Katie Kate took Jimmy to Dr. Swenson's office. Dr. Swenson is a neurologist who helps kids who have epilepsy. It's her job to figure out what kind of epilepsy Jimmy has and what kinds of medicine he needs to control his seizures.

"The first thing Dr. Swenson will do is ask you lots of questions. Just like she's doing here with Susan," said Katie Kate. "Dr. Swenson will ask you how you feel and if you've had seizures before. She will ask you how the seizure felt and how much you remember. Then she will ask your parents if anybody else in your family has ever had epilepsy. She will ask if anyone saw the seizure, and then you will have to take some tests."

"Are the tests hard? Do I get a grade?" said Jimmy.

"Nope, they're not hard at all! For these tests, you just have to follow the doctor's instructions. You're already doing a great job asking questions, Jimmy. See how the Worry Wombat is getting smaller?"

Jimmy and Katie Kate visited Michael, who was taking some of Dr. Swenson's tests.

"What are those things attached to Michael's head?" asked Jimmy.

"Those are electrodes. They help Dr. Swenson see what is going on in Michael's brain. It's part of an EEG test. It checks activity in your brain."

"Does it hurt?"

"It doesn't hurt at all. During the EEG test, Dr. Swenson will videotape a patient's brain while they are in her office."

"So I might be on Dr. Swenson's TV?"

"That's right! Your brain will be famous!" laughed Katie Kate.

"Sometimes Dr. Swenson gives a test called an MRI. Eddie needs an MRI, but not everybody will take this test. The MRI machine helps Dr. Swenson look at pictures of the brain very, very closely.

"Shhhh," whispered Katie Kate. "Be very quiet so we don't ruin the test. Eddie has to lie very still, but the test doesn't hurt at all."

In the next room, Cindy was taking another of Dr. Swenson's tests.

"What's going on with Cindy?" asked Jimmy.

"A nurse is taking some blood from Cindy so that Dr. Swenson can check to make sure that she's healthy in other ways," said Katie Kate.

"Does it hurt?"

"It feels like a quick pinch. It's over before you know it!"

"If you have epilepsy, the doctor will give you medicine. Sometimes it is one or two pills that might keep you from having any more seizures. Sometimes, a person will have to take the medicine for the rest of their life. But there is a chance that when you grow up, you won't have epilepsy anymore."

"Does the medicine taste bad?"

"No way. It's usually just a pill you swallow with some water."

"And that's all I have to do?"

"That's one of the things you have to do. But let's go talk to the other kids about how to stay healthy and safe."

"Taking your medicine is very important," said Katie Kate. "But there are some other things that you can do to help prevent seizures and to protect yourself."

Jimmy listened carefully. "Like what?" he asked.

"The doctor told me that it's very important to get good sleep every night," Michael said. "When you're tired, you are more likely to get a seizure."

Jimmy thought that didn't sound too hard. He was always in bed by bedtime.

"And if you are sick with the flu or a bad cold, you might be more likely to get a seizure, so you have to be careful," said Cindy.

Susan nodded and said, "But if you take your medicine when you're supposed to, you can prevent seizures even when you are sick or tired."

"To make sure you're taking the right amount of medicine, it's important that you get regular checkups with a neurologist like Dr. Swenson," said Katie Kate.

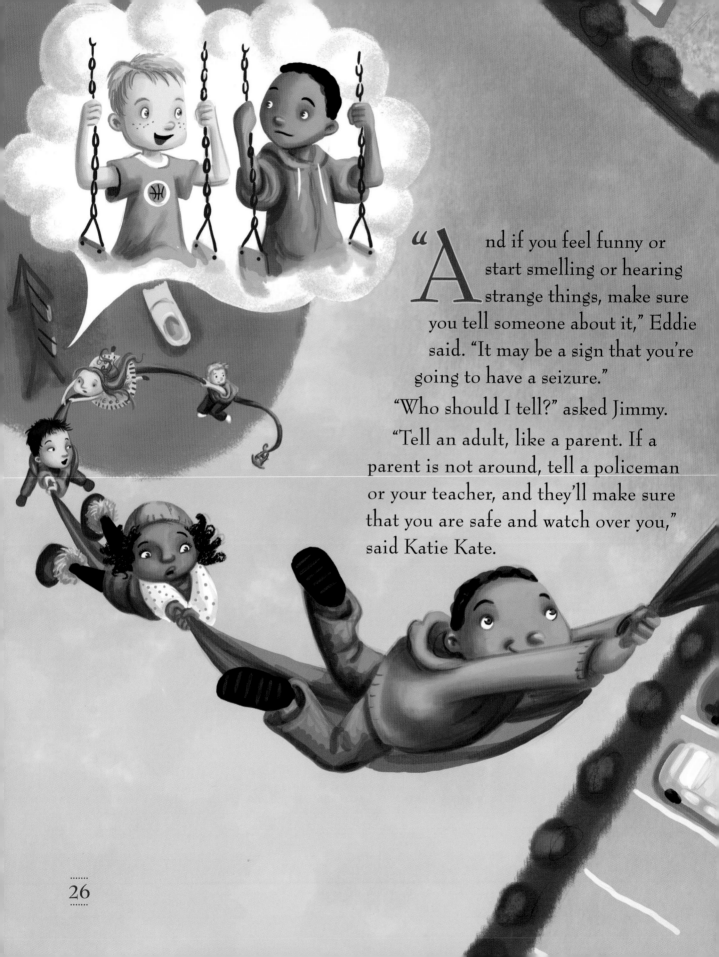

"And if you feel funny or start smelling or hearing strange things, make sure you tell someone about it," Eddie said. "It may be a sign that you're going to have a seizure."

"Who should I tell?" asked Jimmy.

"Tell an adult, like a parent. If a parent is not around, tell a policeman or your teacher, and they'll make sure that you are safe and watch over you," said Katie Kate.

"I can do that," said Jimmy. "Take that, Worry Wombat!"

"Way to go, Jimmy!" cheered Katie Kate. "Now it's time to go back to see Dr. Swenson. Hold on!"

With a twirl of her cape, Katie Kate swept the friends into the air and back to Dr. Swenson's office.

"So Jimmy, what did you learn today about epilepsy?" asked Katie Kate.

"I learned that if we take our medicine, get regular checkups, and get rest, we can do anything we want," Jimmy said.

"That's right," said Katie Kate. "You'll be just like other kids. You just have to take care of yourself."

"I'm not worried anymore."

"Neither are we," said the other kids.

Just then, with a POOF!, the Worry Wombat disappeared.

And so did Katie Kate.

"Where were you?" Jimmy's mother asked.

"Don't worry, Mom," Jimmy said. "I went with Katie Kate and learned all about seizures and epilepsy. And we got rid of the Worry Wombat!"

"Who's Katie Kate? And what's a Worry Wombat?"

The kids all smiled—thanks to The Great Katie Kate.

The End.